AR...

THE HIGHGATE
ESS, ZACK HAS
T TEAM STRIKER
DE THE OTHER
AR MIDFIELDER
S JOSHUA...

HARSH WORLD OF
S MUCH HARDER...

IT'S YOUNG ZACK CASSIDY,
I CAN'T WATCH, TONY!!

GOAALLLLLLL

AND THE COMETS HAVE THEMSELVES A NEW HERO, ZACK CASSIDY, THE NEW NAME ON EVERYONE'S LIPS...

FLOODLIGHT

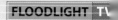

FLOODLIGHT TV

...NOT TO MENTION THE LIPS EVERY GIRL WANTS TO KISS...

ROYSTON ROVERS 3 HIGHGATE COMETS 4

IN RECEPTION...

COME ON JULIE, EVEN THE TV SAYS YOU WANT TO KISS ME...

ZACK, I DON'T DATE FOOTBALLERS.

3

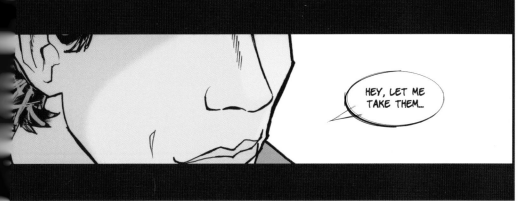

4

OK, TRY THIS - IN MY EXPERIEN YOU FOOTBALLERS ARE QUIT PRETTY BUT THERE ISN'T MUC GOING ON UPSTAIRS. AND NO ONE OF YOU HAS EVEN HEARD OF ROMANCE...

...YOU PROBABLY THINK IT'S A TEAM IN ROME.

NOT ME. I'LL PROVE IT TO YOU. AND WHEN I HAVE, YOU LET ME TAKE YOU OUT, ALRIGHT?

CASSIDY!!

IF YOU'VE QUITE FINISHED, ROMEO, THE BUS IS WAITING!

WE'LL SEE...

...WELL, GRAEME, THE CUP VICTORY AGAINST WESTCHESTER SEEMED TO BE A TURNING POINT FOR THE COMETS.

IN FACT, WITH ALAN SHANE, WES JOSHUA, LUKE PRESTON AND ZACK CASSIDY ALL ON FORM AND SCORING CONSISTENTLY, THE MERSEY FERRYMEN...

...ARE IN FOR A TOUGH AFTERNOON... HA HA!

6

AWAY TEAM

EIDER SVEFFENN 9

HEIGHT	6'
WEIGHT	11 STONE
AGE	24
NATIONALITY	SWEDISH
POSITION	CENTRE FORWARD
WHEELS	SAAB

LAST SEASON

APPEARANCES	37	AGGRESSION	8
GOALS	31	CARDS	1 RED, 5 YELL
GOAL - SHOT RATIO	30	TACKLE	85

SPECIALITY - BALL CONTROL

...AND THE TEAMS ARE COMING OUT. THE BIG NEWS IS THAT CARTER IS GIVING THE OUT OF FORM JED SHANE A START TODAY! WE'RE LEFT WONDERING: IS CARTER TRYING TO GIVE THE KID A LEG UP OR IS IT SIMPLY SQUAD ROTATION? ...MORE SURPRISES FROM THE COMETS TODAY...

15 SHANE J **9** SHANE A

7 JOSHUA **8** SAMPILSON **10** PRESTON **21** DI FLORES

17 FAKAMOTO **6** GOMO **5** DAVIS **2** MONK

13

...FRENCH MIDFIELD STAR RENÉ JUILLET HAS BEEN LEFT ON THE BENCH IN PREFERENCE TO THE SURPRISE CHOICE OF...

TWINRIVERS

...MASSIMO 'MASSY' DI FLORES IN AN ATTACKING RIGHT WING ROLE! THIS'LL BE INTERESTING!

IN THE CHANGING ROOM...

20

LATER, AT THE SPRITZ...

LUKE! LUKE! LUKE!

LUKE! LUKE!

DON'T WORRY, MATE, HAPPENS ALL THE TIME.

ƆOOOM!!

WHAT WOULD YOU LIKE TO DRINK?

I'D LIKE TO SAY A PINT. BUT I DON'T REALLY DRINK.

ME NEITHER, AND THEY DON'T DO PINTS HERE, ZACK. PINTS ARE FOR PUBS, MATE.

HATE THIS SHIR

HI, TWO MINERAL WATERS AND A BOTTLE OF CHAMPAGNE FOR MANDY PLEASE, BARMAN.

YES, SIR. ERR... WOULD YOU SIGN MY NAPKIN PLEASE, MR. PRESTON?

OF COURSE!

24

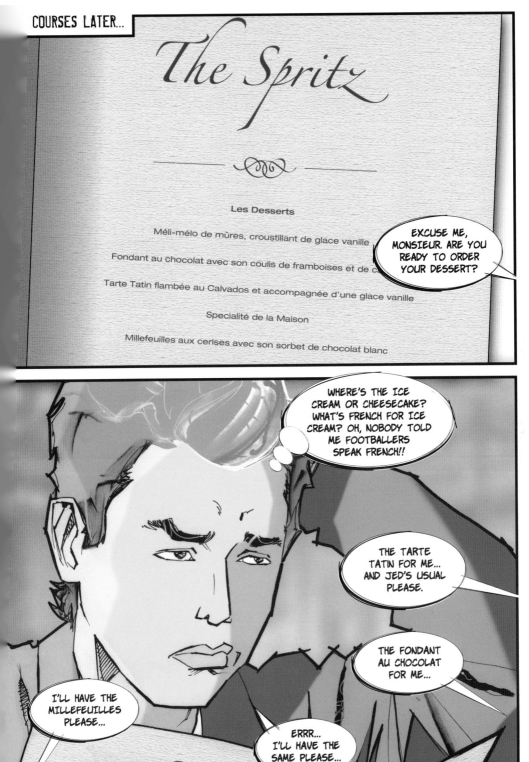

DESSERT ARRIVES...

EXCUSE M[E]
COULD I GET
CHOCOLATE S[AUCE]
PLEASE... HU[RRY]

HI, LUKE.
HI, MANDY.
HI, ALAN.

HEY, BRUCE.
HOW Y'DOIN'?
THIS IS OUR NEW
STRIKER, ZACK...

...CASSIDY.
YEAH, I KNOW, YOU KICKED
BUTT AGAINST ROYSTON.
I HAD THE GAME TAPED FOR
ME AND SENT OVER.

ERR...
ERMM...

ANYWAY, KEEP
UP THE GOOD WORK,
FELLAS. I'LL PICK UP
YOUR CHEQUE.

I DON'T
BELIEVE IT,
B...BRUCE...

BRUCE CANNON
JUST BOUGHT
ME DINNER!!

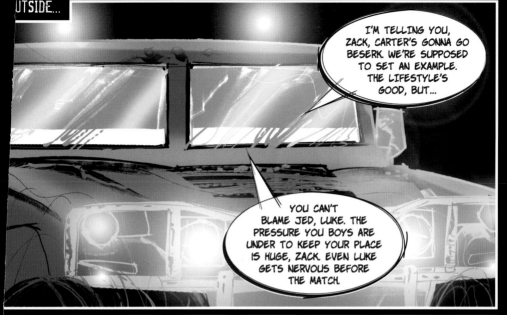

HEE HEE

SNIGGER

SNIGGER

OH WHAT?!

CHAM

CLICK

SSSH! MUM THINKS THEY'VE GONE. WHAT WAS IT LIKE?

GET OUT! YOU'RE ALL MAD!!

SHOVE

ZACK!!

"HOPE THE MORNING'S NOT TOO ROUGH". I DON'T DRINK. WHAT DID HE MEAN?

34

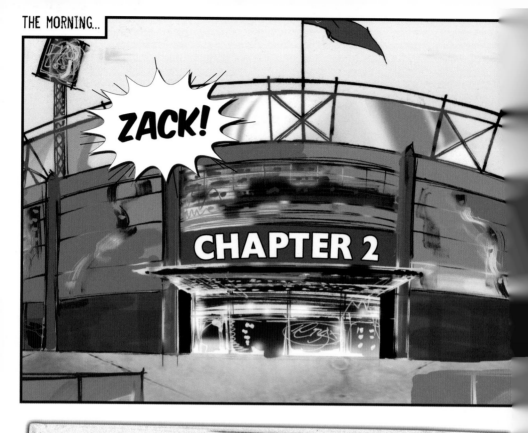

WHADDYA NEED, A NANNY? LOOK AT THESE PAPERS!!!

IT WAS MY FAULT BOSS. ZACK JUST STEPPED IN TO SEPARATE...

WHAT'S WRONG WITH YOU, JED? YOU CAN PUT A DRINK AWAY BUT YOU CAN'T SCORE A GOAL. MAYBE I SHOULD TAPE A CAN OF LAGER TO THE GOALPOST...

RIGHT, WELL, ENOUGH'S ENOUGH!

IN A SHOCK MOVE TODAY, COMETS MANAGER JIM CARTER HAS RESPONDED TO A RESTAURANT FRACAS BY SUSPENDING THE PLAYERS FROM THEIR NEXT MATCH. HERE'S MR. CARTER EARLIER...

GAME OF THE DAY

IN RECEPTION...

I SHOULD MOAN, BUT I CAN SEE HIS POINT.

WELL YOU'RE STILL IN MY BAD BOOKS – TYPICAL FOOTBALLER... DRINKING AND FIGHTING...

AH BUT WHO BRINGS YOU THESE...

HIGHGATE COMETS FC

HIGHGATE COMETS VS NOTTINGHAM ARCHERS

Manager's notes:

With the Ferryman going great guns, every game from now on is a six-pointer, every game counts. But not to the point of our good name, or this club's honour. When I watched the Comets as a kid, I never thought of our players fighting among themselves and I won't have it now. You can blame the media - we'd never have heard about it in all likelihood in my day – or you can blame the pressure, but the bottom line is we're professionals and we're supposed to set an example. My team selection today reflects that belief…

Enjoy the game.

Jim Carter

Jim Carter
Manager

HIGHGATE COMETS

gatecomets.com

Partial left-column text:

6'2"
13 STONE
32
ENGLAND
CENTRE BACK
SUBISHI SHOGUN

ON
GRESSION   10
RDS 5 RED, 11 YELL
CKLE   85

ACKLE, HEADING

you here is quite
of his career now,
erland Sovereigns
covering from a
rn fighter, Chopper
evotion to the team.

g comes close to
tting a little long in
mper which gets
nt off player…

RRRRRRRRRRRRRRRRRRRRRRRRRRRRRRRRRRRRRR

ZACK, I'VE TOLD YOU ABOUT WES, HE'S A WILD ONE. HE'LL GET HIMSELF IN REAL TROUBLE ONE DAY.

I JUST DON'T FEEL I CAN GET ANYTHING RIGHT AT THE MOMENT, ALAN...

RIGHT, BOYS, F.C. COLISEUM ARE SERIOUSLY POWERFUL LADS. NO MESSIN'. WE'RE GOING TO BE LIKE THE COMETS VERSION OF THE S.A.S. – WE GO IN, KICK ARSE AND GET BACK HOME, ALRIGHT? YOU'VE GOT ONE NIGHT OUT ONLY AND I DON'T WANT TO BE PICKING UP THE PIECES, OK?

YES, BOSS!!

INFO ⚽

ITALY - (ITALIA)

FOR MOST OF US THE MOST FAMOUS THING ABOUT ITALY ISN'T PAVAROTTI, OR THE LEANING TOWER OF PIZZA, (SORRY PISA), BUT WHAT'S KNOWN AS 'LA COSA NOSTRA'... THE MAFIA. IMAGINE A WORLD WITHOUT GANGSTER FILMS OR AL PACINO. NOT TO MENTION FERRARIS, ARMANI OR PIZZA FOR THAT MATTER...

SO THIS 'ANTI PASTA'... IS IT, LIKE, THE OPPOSITE OF PASTA? ALWAYS WONDERED...

NO, CHOPPER, YOU MOOK!

YEAH, CHOP, THEY GROW THE SPAGHETTI HERE TOO...

HEY, GUYS, IS THAT...?

ER THE OTHER SIDE...

YEAH, THE TREVI FOUNTAIN - COME ON, WHILE WE'RE WAITING FOR CHOPPER TO GROW A BRAIN...

51

HERE WE ARE, LADS.

WHOA!

SLIIIP!!

ARE YOU OK, ALAN?

DON'T WORRY ABOUT ME, WORRY ABOUT MY ROLEX, MASSY!

OK, I'M OFF TO MEET LUKE AND WES.

PING!

CIAO PAISAN!

SEE YA, MASSY!

DID HE SAY PARMESAN?

SHUDDUP, CHOPPER...

MASSIMO! HEY, MASSY! OVER HERE...

WES! WHAT ARE YOU DOING? COME WITH ME NOW...

TELL ME YOU HAVEN'T..! WE HAVE TO GO, RIGHT NOW!!

60

I DON'T GET IT, WES. YOU SAID YOU NEVER DATE ATTACHED GIRLS!

SHUT UP, ZACK!

MY MAN AT F.C. COLISEUM SAYS FLAVIO'S FIT SO WE'VE GOT EVEN MORE PROBLEMS!

BEEP BEEP BEE

INFO

ROBERTO FLAVIO

"DEADLY WINGER, NUMBER 11. AN ITALIAN RUMOURED TO BE AS FAST, IF NOT FASTER THAN WES. NICKNAMED, NOT TOO AFFECTIONATELY, BY ENGLISH DEFENCES AS, WAIT FOR IT, "GREASER LIGHTNING".

BUT WHILE THE TEAM HEAD TO THEIR GROUND, BOBBY'S MEN HAVE OTHER PLANS...

OK, **NOW!!**

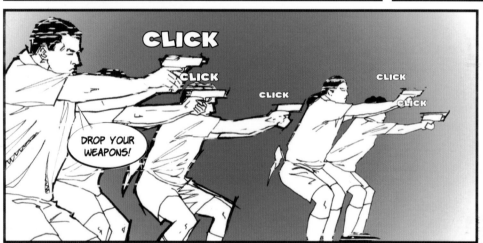

CLICK
CLICK
CLICK
CLICK
CLICK

DROP YOUR WEAPONS!

YOU MEAN REFEREE'S ASSISTANTS, BOSS. NO, THEY ARE MY COUSINS, THE 'SICILY DI FLORES BROTHERS'.

THERE'S TEN OF THEM?

THAT'S ONLY HALF OF THEM, WES!

BUT... OH NO! WHAT'S THIS??!!

WHUMMP!

GAME OF THE DAY

DIVING
WITH CHOPPER DAVIS

"AS A DEFENDER YOU'RE STUCK WITH THIS PROBLEM AND IT'S THE BANE OF YOUR LIFE. I'M NOT EVEN GONNA SAY DIVING IS AN ITALIAN SPECIALITY, LOOK AT ALL THE 'GET-HIT-ON-KNEE BY-BALL-AND-FALL-DOWN-HOLDING-FACE' DIVES AT THE WORLD CUP. YOU'VE GOTTA HOPE THE STRIKERS AREN'T GONNA CHEAT BUT THE ONLY THING YOU CAN DO IS NOT LEAVE ANYTHING FOR THEM TO 'FALL' OVER. BUNCH OF SISSIES, THE LOT OF 'EM."

WHEEEEEEEP!

UP STEPS PAGLICA WITH THE FREE KICK...

OVER IN THE BUSHES...

88

INFO ⚽ RONNIE BIGGS?

"ONE OF THE GREAT TRAIN ROBBERS - NOT SAYING HE WAS A GREAT TRAIN ROBBER, JUST THAT HE WAS ONE OF THE THIEVES IN WHAT WAS KNOWN AS THE GREAT TRAIN ROBBERY, WHICH BECAUSE WE KNOW YOU'RE ASKING - WAS THE STEALING OF MILLIONS FROM A GLASGOW TO LONDON MAIL TRAIN IN 1963. LOOK WALLY'S OLD. HE'S NOT GONNA SAY 'IT'S LIKE LEAVING YOUR GIRLFRIEND WITH WES', IS HE?"

SO, STRAIGHT INSIDE...

91

WELL, IT'S A REAL CASE OF THE GOOD, THE BAD AND THE UGLY OUT THERE...

JUST LIKE IN THE STUDIO, ABI...

COMETS 7   MARAUDERS 0

J SHANE	7, 22, 42
CASSIDY	11, 17
PRESTON	35
JOSHUA	45

GREAT FORM FROM THE COMETS OUT THERE TODAY: JUST LOOK AT THOSE GOALS...

BUT WHAT ON EARTH HAS HAPPENED TO ALAN SHANE? HE'S MAKING SCHOOLBOY ERRORS...

GAME OF THE DAY

YET A HAT TRICK FOR YOUNG JED SHANE - HIS GAME IS REALLY TURNING AROUND.

GAME OF THE DAY

AH, IT'S A CRUEL GAME, PET... RIGHT NOW ALAN'S ABOUT AS HAPPY AS A PENGUIN IN A DESERT...

GAME OF THE DAY

INTO THE SECOND HALF...
KRAKOW!
LISTEN TO THAT, THE HEAVENS HAVE OPENED. CAN THE MARAUDERS PEG ONE BACK?

52 MINUTES...
HERE IT COMES, LADS...
THE COMETS ARE PLAYING AS A TEAM; EVEN THE STRIKERS ARE BACK TO DEFEND, EXCEPT THEIR HUNTER-KILLER OF THE DAY, JED SHANE...
ALAN SHANE... IT'S A HEADER... BUT OH NO!...

HI, GUYS. I GUESS EVERYONE HAS BAD GAMES...

SO, ALAN? NOT REALL YOUR WEEK, IS IT?

AGE FINALLY CATCHIN UP WITH YOU?

12 MISSED SITTERS AN AN OWN GOAL?

SEEMS LIKE EVERYONE IN THE TEAM SCORED EXCEPT YOU?

WOULD YOU SAY YOU'RE NOT SETTING MUCH OF A CAPTAIN'S EXAMPLE?

WOULD YOU SAY THIS IS AN ALL TIME LOW?

WOULD YOU SAY THIS IS ENOUGH TO MAKE YOU THINK ABOUT...

IF HE MENTIONS THE 'R' WORD WE'RE OUT THERE SHARPISH, RIGHT, CHOP?

...RETIREMENT?

SO, WHAT HAPPENED NEXT? WANATHAN'S TEAM...

WELL, NICK THERE'S A STAR ENGLAND PWAYER IN DEFENCE, I MEAN SURELY HE DOESN'T SCORE AN OWN GOAL...

...WHEN HE CAN'T SCORE TO SAVE HIS WIFE!

HA-HA-HA-HA HA HA HA HA

BACK ON THE DATE...

OH NO, THAT BLOKE TALKS LIKE ELMER BLINKIN' FUDD.

OH, THAT'S NOT ALL...

...WHEN ALAN PULLED OUT OF THE STUDIO, HE CRASHED HIS CAR INTO AN ITALIAN ICE CREAM VAN!

INFO — OLD PEOPLE WHO DON'T LIKE BEING CALLED GYPSIES...

"ERRR... THERE'S NOT ACTUALLY THAT MANY OF THEM ABOUT REALLY, BUT ALAN'S ALL OUT OF LUCK AT THE MOMENT..."

MUCH EXPLAINING LATER...

THE COMETS WERE AT HOME AGAIN, THIS TIME TO OLD RIVALS WESTFIELD UTD.

IN THE CHANGING ROOMS...

HE'S THE MANAGER. HE CAN DO ANYTHING HE WANTS.

GAME OF THE DAY

GAME OF THE DAY

HO HO! WELL THANKS, GRAEME. ADAM SPARROW HERE, GLAD TO BE JOINING THE GAME OF THE DAY TEAM. I TELL YOU IT'S AS EXCITING AS A BUCKET OF FROGS DOWN HERE!

GAME OF THE DAY

114

*SEE BOOK ONE

ZACK'S LITTLE SURPRISE...

...AND THE CROWD LOVE IT...

YOU ROCK!

HA HA!

WELL, THE COMETS ARE ON TOP FORM. ALL THAT NEEDS TO BE ASKED IS: CAN SHANE PRODUCE A RABBIT FROM THE CHAPEAU?*

123

*WE THINK HE MEANS A HAT TRICK

HUMMP!

...AND, ON THAT BOMBSHELL OF A GOAL, THE TEAM WELCOME THE CAPTAIN BACK!!

WHAT A GAME FOR THE COMETS! I'LL BET THEY'LL BE CELEBRATING THIS ON NEW YEAR'S EVE...

HIGHGATE COMETS 7:0 WESTFIELD UNITED

YEAR'S EVE AT ZACK AND ROBBIE'S...

5...4...3...2...1...

INFO

ZACK'S PARTY

SORRY, BUT FOR REASONS OF, WELL... DECENCY AND TASTE - CHOPPER WAS THERE REMEMBER - WE CAN'T SHOW YOU EVERYTHING THAT WENT ON AT THE PARTY...

BUT REST ASSURED THEY ALL TURNED UP AND THEY HAD A VERY GOOD TIME...

WHAT'S ROUND THE CORNER FOR THE COMETS?

COMING SOON IN BOOK 3

THE COMETS HAVE SOME TOUGH MATCHES AHEAD OF THEM TO BE IN WITH A CHANCE OF REACHING THE LEAGUE FINAL AND THERE ARE DOUBTS ABOUT LUKE'S FUTURE WHEN MADRID GALACTICOS MAKE A RECORD OFFER FOR HIM. IT COULDN'T COME AT A WORSE TIME, AS RUMOURS OF FINANCIAL TROUBLE PLAGUE THE CLUB - CAN THE COMETS FIND A BUYER OR WILL THEY BE FORCED TO SELL KEY PLAYERS?